BAT BOY

BAT BOY

Paul &
Emma Rogers

Illustrated by Toni Goffe

Dent Children's Books
London

Published in paperback, 1992

First published in 1991
Text copyright © Paul & Emma Rogers, 1991
Illustrations copyright © Toni Goffe, 1991

Printed in Great Britain
by The Guernsey Press Co. Ltd, Guernsey, C.I.
for J. M. Dent & Sons Ltd
Orion House, 5 Upper St Martin's Lane
London WC2

For Toby

1

Desmond was not the kind of boy who had adventures. In fact, there was nothing exceptional about Desmond at all. He was a very ordinary boy of seven – not particularly clever, not especially tall, or fat, or thin. He was a bit short-sighted though, so he wore glasses like his dad.

No, Desmond was not made of the stuff heroes are made of. Life simply seemed to pass him by. He hardly ever got excited about anything.

If you asked Desmond what he did at the weekend, or what presents he got for Christmas, or what he had in his lunchbox, his answer would always be the same: "Nothing much!"

Now it might have been different if he'd had a hero's name – like Indiana or Tarzan. But Desmond's mum and dad didn't watch many films. They were much too busy for that. His mum worked at the library and his dad was a professor at the University. He was an entomologist, which means he was an expert on insects. In his study, alongside the word processor, there was a cupboard with cases full of insects, all dead, lined up in neat rows. Desmond thought they looked disgusting.

On top of the cupboard there was a fox, a squirrel and a bat. They were stuffed. The fox and the squirrel stood in lifelike poses against a painted background in their glass case. The bat just hung upside

down from a stick in his case, with his wings folded. It was as if some bad fairy had come along and, feeling grumpy, had cast a mean and nasty spell on them. Desmond couldn't help feeling a bit sorry for these creatures. He could never resist peering at them, especially at the bat – even though the bat's tiny staring eyes always gave him the creeps.

Once, Desmond carried the bat down to the kitchen to show it to the French girl, Celine. She looked after Desmond's baby brother, Sam. Celine never said much to Desmond. But when she saw the bat she screamed and screamed. Sam thought this was very funny. He sat in his highchair gurgling and clapping. Then he tipped his lunch all over the floor.

When Desmond's mum came home, Celine was still trembling. She pointed at Desmond and explained about "Zee 'orrid leetle creeture!" Desmond got such a telling off he promised himself he'd never ever speak to Celine in future.

All in all, Desmond didn't think having a baby brother was much fun. Sam had just learned to crawl. Sometimes he got into places he wasn't meant to, while Celine talked on the phone to her friends. Now and then, Desmond tried to play a game with him, but somehow Sam always ended up sitting on the floor flapping his arms and making squeaking noises.

"Huh!" Desmond sighed to himself, "I might as well try playing with that bat!"

As for Desmond's older brother and sister – well, they were always busy. They were either studying for exams in their rooms or studying their spots in the bathroom mirror.

When Desmond wandered in they'd snap at him: "Clear off! Stop hanging around where you're not wanted!"

So Desmond was left pretty well to himself. He simply got on with being Desmond without anyone interfering.

Occasionally his parents might say something like: "Have you washed your ears recently, Desmond?" or "You have to go to the optician's this afternoon. Celine will take you."

But most of the time Desmond lived a quiet, uneventful life – which was how he liked it.

At school too, he did his best not to get noticed. He sat in a desk next to the window, his head resting on his fist, day-dreaming.

One day Desmond's teacher, Mr Gosling, said: "Now Class 3, tell me, what do you know about castles?"

There was a moment's silence. Then Mr Gosling picked on Desmond.

"Well Desmond," he said, "What do you know about castles?"

You can guess what Desmond answered: "Nothing much."

Jason Freeman, who sat behind Desmond, called out: "I know sir – they're boring!"

Class 3 giggled. Jason always had an answer for everything.

Mr Gosling ignored Jason and went on: "Well – you're soon going to know a lot about castles because I've chosen Chumley Castle for our class outing."

Class 3 groaned. Everyone had been hoping their outing this term would be to the zoo. Mr Gosling had all but promised they might go when they were doing their project on flying. Even Desmond, who had chosen "Creatures of the Night" and had written three whole pages on owls and bats and things like that, had been sort of looking forward to it.

Mr Gosling tried to tempt Class 3, "It's a very well-preserved castle, with a drawbridge and a moat! Turrets! A kitchen – with all the old cooking equipment, though nobody lives there now. And – oh yes – a splendid heraldry display!" Everyone groaned again. Then Jason put up his hand.

Mr Gosling sensed trouble as he muttered, "Yes Jason – what is it?"

"Will there be any dungeons, sir? And a Chamber of Horrors?"

"Well if there is," snapped Mr Gosling, "We'll arrange to leave you there, Jason. Tell your mother you might not make it home tomorrow evening."

Everybody laughed, then cheered. Jason grinned at his audience.

Unlike Desmond, Jason did have a hero's name and he certainly tried to live up to it. Whenever

there was any excitement, or fun, or mischief to be had – you can bet Jason would be in the middle of it. He even had a gang he called "The Argonauts". To join it, you had to swear a solemn oath and promise always to be naughty. Desmond had meant to join – but somehow he'd never got round to it.

At the end of school, Mr Gosling said, "Now remember. Everybody here by 8.30. We want to make sure we get off to a flying start!"

2

"**W**ow!" said Jason. "What a place to live!"

Mr Gosling proudly led Class 3 over the wood-wormed drawbridge. And even Desmond had to admit it – Chumley Castle, with its four massive towers, its battlements and deep green moat was better than he'd expected.

"Now remember," said Mr Gosling. "We have to keep together. We're a party."

"Doesn't feel like a party to me!" whispered Jason to Desmond as Mr Gosling handed over the tickets to a big, grumpy-looking lady in the kiosk.

"Good morning Mrs Best," said Mr Gosling. "Here we are. All present and correct!"

Mrs Best stared, rather menacingly, over her desk at Jason and Desmond, as Mr Gosling handed out the worksheets to Class 3.

"Right. Question number one," said Mr Gosling. "What is the building you see after crossing the drawbridge?"

Desmond squinted. The sun was dazzling on his glasses. But beyond the gateway he spotted a sign saying "KEEP". That was it! He'd heard of castles having keeps. Pressing the worksheet on his leg, he wrote down the answer. Several others, including Jason, copied it. Then they followed Mr Gosling into the castle yard, passing the sign:

Jason was already on it. And Desmond, without thinking, had gone after him.

"Jason! Desmond! Come here at once!" yelled Mr Gosling, glancing over his shoulder towards the kiosk. "That's a good start, isn't it? You two can stick close to me for the rest of the visit!"

He herded them into the castle library. More questions. Desmond yawned. His pen kept puncturing the paper, making blue spots all over his leg. After the library, there was the heraldry exhibition. After the heraldry exhibition, there was the kitchen. Then they all trooped into the banqueting room. Desmond sighed and began to wonder what the time was.

"Lunch-time!" called Jason, grinning from one end of the long polished table.

Mr Gosling glanced at his watch and said, with relief, "Indeed it is! Now listen everybody. First stop is the washrooms. And remember – stick together – we're a–"

But no one in Class 3 heard him say "party". No one, that is, except Desmond. He had spotted a magnificent stag's head up on the wall above the fireplace. It was stuffed – like the creatures in his dad's study.

"You too, Desmond!" said Mr Gosling. "Stop day-dreaming!'

Hastily Desmond scuttled off after the rest of Class 3.

But by the time he reached the washroom in the basement, most of them were leaving. Only a few stragglers remained behind, splashing water at each other and playing with the automatic dryers. When Desmond came out of his cubicle, even they had disappeared.

Quickly, he washed his hands, his worksheet clamped between his knees. Then he hurried out into the corridor. There was no sign of Mr Gosling or any of Class 3, but Desmond could guess where they had gone. Or, at least, he thought he could.

He climbed the stone stairs two at a time and came to a landing. Not that way, he thought, for the corridor was roped off. There was another flight of stairs on Desmond's left.

"Ah well," he sighed as he began to climb. His footsteps echoed. His tummy rumbled loudly as he carried on up the silent stairway. Desmond was getting very hungry. He couldn't remember its being this far, or this gloomy. But then, being Desmond, he might simply not have noticed the first time.

"Where was that banqueting room?" he whis-

pered to himself. His heart had begun to beat just a little bit anxiously.

"If the others aren't up here," Desmond declared when he was half-way there, "I'll turn back."

And that's exactly what he would have done if he hadn't spotted the wooden door at the top of yet another flight of steps. So up he went.

At the top he stopped to catch his breath.

"Perhaps this is an office or something," he whispered outside the door, though it looked rather dusty for that. There were masses of thick, sticky cobwebs hanging everywhere.

"Oh heck," said Desmond, who didn't like the look of things. "I'd better see where this goes to. Mr Gosling will be furious with me if I don't get back!

He lifted his hand and tapped nervously. No one answered so Desmond tried banging with his fist. There was still no answer so he grabbed the iron latch and rattled it. The heavy door swung open with a low groan.

It was not an office after all. It was some sort of store room. There was loads of clutter – boxes and books, old tables and chairs, and even a rusty suit of armour.

It was the suit of armour that did it. Desmond couldn't resist taking a closer look. So he stepped into the room and – BANG! – the door slammed shut behind him.

3

"**W**ell?" a voice snapped. "Who are you?"

Desmond looked round. An old woman, draped in black, was standing behind him. Her face was a horrid pale grey – like cold porridge. Her prune-black eyes glinted beneath red lids. And the finger that pointed straight at him was more like a claw – long-nailed, crooked and warty. Desmond shivered.

An icy fear gripped him and something inside was saying: "Don't bother explaining. Don't even ask the way back. Just get out of here. Quick."

But he couldn't. She was between him and the doorway.

Suddenly, she jumped towards him, wagging her finger, warts and all.

"I suppose you're another of those interfering busybodies – coming in here, disturbing my peace!"

Desmond shook his head vigorously. He opened his mouth. He tried to speak but nothing came out. Not even a squeak.

"What's the matter?" she snarled. "Cat got your tongue or something?"

Desmond glanced desperately into the room behind. High up on a ledge there was a big cat staring, slitty-eyed, straight at him. Desmond had the feeling something nasty was going to happen. Something very, very nasty. Oh, if only he'd stuck with the rest of Class 3!

The woman was so close to him now he could see bits of spit on her crusty old lips.

"Last chance!" she threatened him. "Now or never! Speak! What does a little wretch like you want in here?"

Desmond gulped. He shuffled his feet.

"Me?" he mumbled. "Oh – nothing much, really."

"NOTHING MUCH!" shrieked the woman. "Nothing much indeed!" She sprang towards him, sending up eddies of ancient dust. "Now you listen to me – I'll give you nothing much you miserable little creature!"

Suddenly there was a lightning flash. And a bang like thunder. The whole room seemed to be moving. The last thing Desmond saw before he shut his eyes was the room tilting to one side. It was like being on a ship in a terrible storm. Then he felt a wind whipping round his shorts. Next thing, he had flipped upside down and was hanging from a beam in the ceiling.

Desmond felt sick. He also felt the blood surge into his head, like it did when he swung upside down on the school climbing frame. Then he would hang by the crook of his knees. Now it felt as if he was hanging on with his feet. This can't be happening to me – it's a bad dream, thought Desmond. But when he opened his eyes he really was hanging upside down. And to his dismay, everything around

him – shapes and colours – had merged into a fuzzy blur.

"Oh heck!" said Desmond, "I've lost my specs!"

He lifted his hands to his face to check. His arms unfolded like an umbrella. He closed them again, tightly to his sides. And what a surprise – his body was completely covered in velvety fur.

Whatever's the matter? thought Desmond, I must be going batty!

Suddenly, he knew it. Something terrible *had* happened. Something really drastic. He was no longer Desmond, the ordinary boy of seven. He was a *bat*!

The shock nearly made Desmond drop from his beam. Only those powerful toes, and the extra hooks on his wings, prevented him from crashing down among the heaps of dusty junk below. WINGS! Desmond could hardly believe what had happened to him. He hung there for a while, miserably silent. He felt like crying. If this was an adventure then Desmond could do without it.

Meanwhile, somewhere beneath him, the old woman was muttering, "Nasty noisy kids! Hoards

of horrible tourists! Who needs them! Why can't they leave me in peace? It's all the fault of that Mrs Best and her stupid committee. Always trying to improve the place and make more money! Anyone can see it's all right as it is. But bossy old Best says Chumley needs more visitors. Huh! What rubbish!"

The odd thing was that although she was mumbling only to herself as she paced up and down the room, Desmond could hear every word of it – very clearly. And it was also clear that he had made a terrible mistake. Why had he not noticed before?

This old woman was a witch! No doubt about it. How stupid of him not to have guessed! After all, she was wearing a black dress (very cobwebby) and long black boots (twice as big as Desmond's dad's). Her black hat (tall and pointed) and black cloak (very tatty) were hanging from a hook next to a long broomstick just like the ones Desmond had seen in books. And there were other clues — her

hair for instance. Wasn't it rather stringy and straggly and a curious shade of green?

"Ah well," sighed Desmond gloomily, "too late now."

Just then, the witch flopped into one of the rickety chairs. It creaked and groaned and Desmond peered into the shadows, trying to see what she was doing. Everything was quiet. The witch was thinking.

Then Desmond's sensitive ears caught another sound – a rustling and a whispery footstep. The cat was stretching herself on her ledge.

A throaty, rumbly voice said, "Take no notice of herrr. She's got a drrreadful temperrr."

Desmond thought he could see the eyes of the cat narrowing slowly.

"Excuse me," he said. His voice sounded high-pitched and squeaky. "Did you just speak to me?"

The cat replied, "Cerrrtainly I did."

"So," said Desmond. "Let me get this right. I can understand you – and you can understand me?"

"Perrrfectly!"

Desmond gasped. Was he really chatting to a cat?

"Don't be daft," he murmured. Then he decided to try it again. But before he had time to say anything –

"QUIET UP THERE!" the witch screamed. "Some of us need our beauty sleep!"

4

Unlike the witch, Desmond didn't feel the slightest bit sleepy. After all, he hadn't really got into a bat's routine yet. So he watched the afternoon sunlight fade. He saw the moonlight slowly take its place. And the later it got, the more wide awake Desmond became. Outside an owl was calling, while down below, the witch was snoring.

Desmond was feeling a bit dizzy though – being rather new to this hanging business too. He clung on to his beam as best he could, alert and listening. Every little sound – the cat's steady breathing, the

witch's chair creaking, even a spider's scuttling – was picked up by Desmond's super-sharp ears.

Suddenly he heard the witch stirring down below. She yawned.

"Ah yes!" she said. "That's much better. Nothing like a good day's sleep to get you thinking more clearly."

What a relief, thought Desmond. At least she doesn't seem quite so angry!

The witch reached for her cloak and rammed on her hat. Then, glancing up at the ceiling where Desmond was hanging, she said to him, "I shouldn't get too comfortable up there if I were you. We'll soon be leaving."

"Leaving?" squeaked Desmond.

He dug his toes into the beam and gripped tightly with his wing hooks. He'd just got used to being there. Now she was talking about leaving! Desmond wrapped the leathery wing-skin round his face.

"I'm not going anywhere," he squeaked.

The cat looked up. "Haven't you hearrrd?" she murmured to Desmond. "This castle is being up-grrraded. Mrs Best is orrrganising lots of imprrrrove-ments. Take this rrroom, forrr instance ..."

"What about it?" said Desmond, peeping out from his wings.

"It's going to be the new inforrrmation centrrre for the castle museum," the cat explained, "with maps and books and historrrical documents to be used by lots of childrrren, like you–"

"Like I used to be, you mean," interrupted Desmond, gloomily.

He might have hung there in this mood for the rest of the evening but it was not to be. Suddenly he found things taking a turn for the worse!

While he had been talking to the cat, the witch had grabbed her broomstick and climbed onto the chair beneath him.

"Come on!" she yelled. "Everybody out!"

And with that, she clouted Desmond on the head with the prickly end of her broomstick.

"Your arrival's convinced me," she said. "As long as I stay here I'm sure to be plagued with visitors. So we're going to find somewhere else to live. Somewhere dark and lonely! Somewhere miserably gloomy! Somewhere no one will ever want to visit!"

She swung the broomstick again. The next swipe got him smack in the chest. Desmond clung on tighter than ever, swinging from side to side like a pendulum.

"Hey! What are you doing?" he squeaked, as the third blow stung him on the toes. He clung on for a moment longer and then he let go! With a piercing little shriek, he slipped from the beam and hooked onto one of the broomstick's bristles.

"Stupid creature!" hissed the witch, as she brought the broomstick crashing down – and Desmond with it. The cat sprang from the ledge and scampered into the shadows in the corner of the room. She looked on with wide green eyes as Des-

mond tightened his grip on the broomstick's bristles and prepared for the worst.

"Whoever heard of a bat that's scared of flying!" the witch screeched.

She shook the broomstick angrily. Then gave up trying to dislodge him and swung her leg over it.

"Well, cling on there if you must. But like it or not – you're coming with me!"

Desmond felt the broomstick tremble. They were off – heading straight for the open window. His stomach lurched, just as it used to on the big dipper. For a second the memory of Class 3's "Flying" project flashed through his mind. They'd seen a film which was supposed to show what it was like being a bird in full flight.

"But it wasn't like this," groaned Desmond, as the freezing wind whistled in his ears.

"Wheee!" shrieked the witch. "Yipeee!"

They were climbing – higher and terrifyingly higher. Desmond closed his eyes. He felt decidedly queasy and clung onto the broomstick feverishly. Roof-tops, shooting stars, the milky-white moon – Desmond missed all these things.

"Well?" the witch cackled over her shoulder. "Fun isn't it?"

Desmond couldn't answer. He was too busy concentrating on not being sick. After a few minutes (which felt like ages), his ears noticed a new sound.

A shrill voice, close to him, squeaked, "Good evening. Nice night for flying."

Desmond dared to open his eyes. Even from this extraordinary angle, he recognized the church steeple, though he had never been as close as this before. Then he peered at the creature gliding alongside the broomstick. It was a bat, just like him. For a moment Desmond forgot his fears and smiled.

He looked around and saw that there were more of them, all silhouetted against the night sky. They came flitting out of the belfry and swooped and soared in the moonlight. It looked so exciting, even Desmond felt tempted to try.

But there wasn't time. For just then, the broomstick made a steep dive.

5

"**H**old on tight!" screamed the witch.

Hold on tight? thought Desmond. He couldn't have held any tighter if he'd tried.

The broomstick swept over the roof of a large farmhouse. Desmond's end clipped the cockerel on the weathervane, sending it spinning dizzily. Then they brushed past a cluster of trees, swerved suddenly and landed.

Desmond sighed with relief. His heart was thumping in his furry chest.

"Oh when will all this end?" he murmured.

"It has ended," snapped the witch, "for the time being."

She swung her leg stiffly over the broomstick.

"Now if I'm not mistaken – there's an old barn somewhere round here. People are always turning them into homes these days – it might be quite cosy."

She set off, dragging the broomstick behind her. Desmond clung on to it, bouncing and bumping over the cobbled farmyard. Up ahead was a huge cowshed. Desmond could hear the animals inside shifting about uneasily.

The wooden door creaked open. Desmond squinted into the gloom. Big shadowy beasts loomed over the stalls on either side. The witch stepped forward to get a better view.

"MOOO!" said the cow next to Desmond. "No rooom!"

"All right! All right!" said the witch. "Keep your horns on. I can see that already. Anyway," she added, "I couldn't stand the smell. Too natural and healthy!"

She dragged the broomstick (and Desmond) back outside. The barn door banged shut behind her.

Then, on the opposite side of the yard, the sheepdog opened his eyes. He sprang to his feet and barked from the doorway of his kennel. His chain

jangled noisily. A light went on in an upstairs window of the house but the broomstick, carrying Desmond and the witch, was already soaring over the chimneys.

Soon they had left the farm and the fields way behind and were heading towards the town where Desmond used to live.

"I must be getting really desperate!" screamed the witch. "Looking for a place to live amongst all these people!"

In fact, at that moment, Desmond couldn't see

anything. He was feeling giddy again and had folded his wings over his face. He was like a little leather parcel hidden between the broomstick's bristles.

Down below, the signs outside the petrol station on the edge of the town sparkled cheerfully and a string of street lights glowing orange in the dark guided the witch into the High Street.

"What a lot of useless clutter." she muttered, as the broomstick sped past a row of shops. "No place like home here ... But what about that?"

The broomstick slowed. Desmond parted his wings and peered out. They were circling the Town Hall, with its twin towers, flying buttresses and all.

"Looks pretty quiet. Shall we try it?" said the witch. Then she noticed the Police Station across the road. It was bathed in blue light from the lamp over the doorway.

"Perhaps not!" she decided and the broomstick shot upwards again, like a silent rocket.

On and on they flew. Looping in wide circles over the town until suddenly they were plummeting downwards again.

"Oh no!" squeaked Desmond. "Her engine's cut out!"

Fearing the worst, he braced himself to hit the earth. The past few hours of his life flashed through his tiny mind and he found himself wishing: "Oh why didn't I stick with the rest of Class 3!"

BUMP! They landed safely and skidded to a halt alongside some iron railings.

"Now this looks more like it!" the witch shrieked.

Once more, Desmond sighed with relief. He was trembling. His head was spinning. And yet, as he fixed his blurry gaze upon the two big iron gates, he had the feeling that there was something familiar about this place. Something he recognized ...

The gates were locked. No problem! The broomstick, with Desmond and the witch, simply hopped over them.

"Mmmm!" said the witch approvingly. "Nice tall railings all round the property, to keep out unwelcome callers. And not too much in the way of a garden to look after."

She dragged the broomstick and Desmond over the tarmac.

"A nice big yard." she said. "And look! How intriguing!"

She pointed at the red and yellow lines painted on the ground.

"Magic marks I expect. I'll look them up in my books when we get back to the castle."

For Desmond, the feeling that all this was very familiar was growing stronger and stronger.

"And look at this!" cried the witch. "Double doors. Double lock – and blinds on every window! It's splendid! Splendid!"

"Oh heck!" said Desmond. Yes! It had dawned on him. This was the front entrance to his school.

"You can't live here!" he piped up.

"Why not?" snapped the witch. "It's empty isn't it? Are you telling me someone lives here already?"

"Well no ..." began Desmond.

"Of course not!" said the witch. "It's deserted. Just like the castle was when I first took up residence! Well, they won't catch me out a second time. Once we get settled in here, I'll put a spell on the place. As well as those railings, I'll have an enchanted forest, fifty metres thick. Then no one – no one at all – will ever be able to bother me!"

6

Desmond tried to explain: "A school's no place for a witch to live!"

But the witch was not listening. She was excited. She was happy even. She skipped onto her broomstick and, with Desmond still clinging to the bristles, she headed back to the castle to sort out all her belongings.

"It may be empty now," said Desmond, his little voice battling with the wind. "But in the morning it's different. It's filled with people then – over two hundred children, not to mention the teachers!"

"Stop squeaking!" called the witch over her shoulder. "A school did you say? Good! The perfect place! There's a whole lot of things you need to learn! How to fly, for instance – "

The broomstick zipped along a line of roof-tops and zigzagged between the chimney-pots. Desmond clung on, tighter than ever.

"I don't believe this," he groaned. "I must be dreaming!"

Just then, they whizzed past an attic bedroom window.

"Hey stop!" yelled Desmond.

In the pinkish light of early morning, he got a blurry glimpse of a Lego model on the window-sill.

Behind it there was a blue-striped duvet on a bed. Desmond was sure he recognized it. Yes! They were flying directly over his own house!

"STOP!" he cried again. "Look!"

He waved a wing, for a moment forgetting he was riding on the broomstick. Next second he was dropping down, down, down. And the ground of his own back garden was rising to meet him.

It was instinct that saved him.

"Help!" he yelled. "Help, someone! Save me!" and in a desperate gesture he flung his arms apart.

As if by magic, his wings opened wide on each side of him. They spread like a parachute and Desmond was no longer falling. He was gliding! Next, he tried a bit of flapping. Then some swooping and turning. Soon he was cruising smoothly over the roof-tops – right past his own bedroom window.

"I'm flying! I'm flying!"

"About time too," said the witch from alongside him.

"Look at me! Look at me!" cried Desmond to the birds who were just waking up in the conker tree at the corner of the street. "PING!" the sound of his voice came bouncing back to him.

Of course! Bats fly with echoes, he thought. And as the "pings" and "beeps!" filled his ears, he flew with perfect accuracy between two T.V. aerials,

skimmed over some telephone wires and dived low into his own back garden. If only they knew, thought Desmond, as he flitted past the curtained windows, behind which he guessed his family were sleeping cosily.

Suddenly, Desmond felt a bit homesick – and more than a bit sorry for himself. Suddenly, as he thought of his mum and dad, his brothers and sister, he felt a warm, fond feeling in his tummy and the prick of a tear in his eye. Yes, it was true! He was even missing Sam and Celine! How he wished he could just be ordinary old Desmond again ... and then he remembered.

"Huh!" he said glumly. "If Celine saw me now, she'd probably scream. As for the rest of them, I don't suppose they've even noticed I'm missing yet!"

This was not that far from the truth. For yesterday, the day of the visit to Chumley Castle, Desmond's mum was at her woodwork class all evening while his dad played chess at the university.

"I bet they think I'm in bed – fast asleep!" said Desmond, and, thinking of sleep, Desmond did begin to feel terribly weary.

"Come along then!" the witch yelled. She was hovering on her broomstick over the street. "I'm starving! Let's get going!"

There was nothing else for it. Desmond could hardly go into his own home for something to eat, could he? So he flew on behind the broomstick, all the way back to the castle.

The witch shot through the open window, landed and hurled the broomstick into the corner with a clatter.

"Breakfast!" she squawked, waking up the cat.

"Brrreakfast?" purred the cat. "Sounds marrrvellous!"

She stretched, arched her back and narrowed her eyes happily at Desmond. He was hanging from his beam again, his tired wings folded neatly. At this mention of breakfast, his little tummy rumbled. He was feeling extremely peckish as well as tired. After all, it had been a whole day and a night since he'd last eaten anything.

He was just wondering what bats eat for breakfast when he heard a loud scuttling and scrabbling, coming from the corner over by the cat.

"Herrre you arrre! Trrry this forrr starrrterrrs." she called up to him.

Desmond hesitated before answering. "Who? Me do you mean?"

The cat sprang up onto her ledge and reached towards Desmond with one paw. There was something tiny wriggling in her claws. Desmond squinted hard and sniffed.

"What is it?" he asked.

"It's forrr yourrr brrreakfast! A rrreally scrrrumptious crrreature! Herrre, take it!" said the cat.

Desmond shuddered.

"Of courrrse," said the cat. "I underrrstand. You preferrr things caught on the wing! Well, this moth

40

was rrresting in the cornerrr. But it's still alive. See, its wings arrre twitching!"

Poor thing! Desmond thought. He could remember what it felt like, catching moths in your hand, their wings fluttering and tickling.

Meanwhile, the witch was busying about down below. She poured some milk for the cat, lit a little camping stove and stirred something in a saucepan. A very nasty smell drifted upwards. The cat, however, didn't seem to mind. She took a deep sniff and sighed approvingly. If it's scrambled eggs, thought Desmond, they're rotten!

After a minute or two, the witch screeched, "Come and get it!"

Does she mean me? Desmond was worried! Perhaps that moth wasn't such a bad idea after all!

The cat, anxious to get down to her smelly breakfast, was waving the insect impatiently towards him. Desmond had no choice but to take it (still warm) in his claws. To his great astonishment his mouth began to water. Suddenly he thought of all those insects in the display cases in his dad's study.

Once, when he'd screwed up his nose in distaste, his dad had said, "Don't be so squeamish, Desmond! Lots of people eat insects."

It had made Desmond feel sick. Closing his eyes, Desmond lifted the moth to his mouth. It felt soft and squashy – except for the crunchy wing bits. Instinct told Desmond to spit these out. Then – in a split second – he gulped and swallowed the rest.

"Hey!" said Desmond in surprise. "That's not bad! It's quite nice!"

The cat smiled and Desmond was just thinking about asking her to catch him some seconds, when a little gnat buzzed by.

"PING!" Desmond's echo was working. In a flash he had swooped down and swallowed that too. Hmmm, he thought, when he was back on his beam, I'm beginning to get the hang of this!

He was straining his ears, hoping to catch the swish of another passing insect, when, "Settle down up there!" bellowed the witch, nearly deafening him. "It's time to get some sleep. We've got a busy night ahead. It's going to take lots of flights to transfer all our things to the new place!"

7

Desmond was awoken early – early for a bat, that
is. It was around midday. Strange voices came drift-
ing up the stairs.

One in particular, loud and bossy, called, "Come
along everybody! This way! Dusters at the ready!"

There were footsteps outside. Then the doorlatch
clicked. A bunch of people shuffled into the room,
led by the lady from the castle kiosk – Mrs Best.

Desmond looked about anxiously. There was no
sign of the witch or of the cat. The broomstick,
cloak and hat had gone and bright sunlight shone
through the open window.

"Dear oh dear!" someone was saying. "It's a long
time since anyone did any spring cleaning in here!"

"Exactly!" agreed Mrs Best. The corners of her
mouth drooped grimly and she had folded her arms
on her chest. Even upside down, Desmond recognized her immediately. Big and dangerous, thought
Desmond. She'd looked just the same when she was
collecting the tickets.

"All right then troops!" said Mrs Best, rolling
up her sleeves and revealing a pair of powerful bi-
ceps. She eyed her helpers like a general inspecting
his army.

"Let's get on with it and attack this mess."

Oh no! thought Desmond as a lot of crashing
and banging began down below. Now he could guess

why the witch had left so suddenly. Years of dirt and peace were shattered. Desmond pulled his wings in closely, hoping that, if he was perfectly still, no one would notice him. Great clouds of dust puffed upwards. Mrs Best and the members of her committee were heaving all the furniture and bits and pieces to one side of the room.

"ATISHOO!" spluttered Desmond.

"Bless you!" said Mrs Best. She didn't even look up to see who had sneezed. She was too busy rummaging among the witch's belongings. "What dusty old books! And a gas stove too! Whatever is that doing here?"

If only she knew, thought Desmond, shuffling even further into his corner. Against the dark brown wood of the beam he was quite well camouflaged. At least so far, so good!

Mrs Best was shaking out her dusters now.

"To battle everybody! Into those nasty corners!" While the committee members got busy, Mrs Best turned her attention to the ceiling.

"Look at all those cobwebs!" she shrieked. "There's only one thing for them!"

Seconds later, Desmond heard a dreadful, ear-shattering clatter. This was followed by a click then a ROAR! Whatever was it? Some hunger-mad

monster? Desmond shuddered, but when he dared to risk one blurry glance, he saw that Mrs Best was brandishing the castle vacuum cleaner. With teeth clenched and eyes narrowed determinedly, she began attacking the swags of cobwebs in the corner nearest the door.

Desmond huddled into his wings and began praying, "Please don't start on this beam ..."

The snorting, sucking, snake-like end of the vacuum cleaner was coming closer and closer.

Suddenly, a terrible force was snatching and tearing at Desmond. He knew he would have to act quickly if he was going to save his furry skin and escape.

Squeaking fearfully, Desmond spread his wings and flung himself from the beam. Aiming for the open window he sailed straight and low over Mrs Best's head. The effect was spectacular.

"HELP!" screamed Mrs Best. "Help! There's a bat in here!"

She lashed at Desmond with the end of the vacuum cleaner. He swerved and ducked and beat his wings furiously.

"This is it!" he gasped. "This is the end! It's going to swallow me!"

He felt the vacuum cleaner's hot breath on his cheek and above its beastly roar, he heard Mrs Best shrieking.

"Get it out! Get it out! Do something! Quickly!"

Mrs Best was waving the vacuum cleaner crazily. Her face had turned a pale greenish colour. At the same time she began to stagger across the room. Then, to everyone's astonishment, she fainted! Desmond felt the room shake as she landed on her back and the vacuum cleaner crashed down with her. Of course! Desmond knew it there and then! For all her fierceness, Mrs Best was as terrified of bats as Celine had been!

He didn't hang about to see what would happen next, but as he flew through the open window, he couldn't help hearing one of the committee members saying, "Well I'm blowed! Bats eh? Now Mrs Best's improvement plan is going to have to change!"

8

Desmond did not give a thought to where he was going. He just kept on flying, thrilled by the feel of fresh air on his face and the wind in his ears.

"I'm alive! I'm alive" he squeaked with relief.

Bit by bit though, he began to calm down. His little heart settled to a steady beat and he started thinking.

"This doesn't feel right!" he said aloud, peering at the blue sky flecked with clouds. "Bats like me should be fast asleep in broad daylight!"

"PING!" There was a building up ahead. Perhaps he could find some shelter? Silently and speedily, he flitted into the church belfry.

It was cool and dark inside. Almost tomblike. All around Desmond, huddled in neat little clumps on the wall, the belfry bats were sleeping. Desmond could hear them breathing softly. Taking care not to disturb any of them, he squeezed into a corner by an old jackdaw's nest. The last thing Desmond noticed before his eyes closed was the big church bell hanging heavy and still beneath him ...

It only seemed like minutes later when a terrifying DONG! DONG! split Desmond's ears. He woke with such a start that he very nearly dropped off the wall. In fact, Desmond had been asleep for hours. Night was falling and the big church bell was calling people to the evening service.

"Bit of a shock, eh?" giggled the bony little bat next to Desmond. "Always an early start for us bats on Wednesdays. Same on Sundays."

"You're joking!" said Desmond, who'd never liked being woken up at the best of times. Still a bit disorientated, he spread his wings and launched himself into the black, flapping cloud of bats.

"I say!" said the little bat again. "Wasn't it you that I almost bumped into last night? You were riding on the broomstick with the witch."

"That's right!" replied Desmond as he recognized the friendly voice from yesterday evening.

"Dearie me!" his new friend squeaked. "I don't envy you living with her! Bit of a tyrant, isn't she?"

They were flying over the farm. A light glowed cosily in the barn. Ahead was the town. Desmond saw it twinkling, like a huge, friendly Christmas tree.

"Actually, I don't live with her," said Desmond. "Not any more anyway. We've all just been driven out of our old home in the castle – the cat, the witch and me. And the witch has got some daft idea into her head about setting up house in a school down there."

"I see," murmured the other bat, thoughtfully. Desmond didn't bother to add that the school in question was *his* school. How could he possibly explain that to a bat?

"Anyway," Desmond went on "I wouldn't dream of going with her. Especially since she says she's going to put some horrible spell on the place! So there you are. I don't belong anywhere really."

Desmond gulped back the tears and flew on miserably. There was a moment when all he could hear was a chorus of all the other bats squeaking and wings beating.

Then his friend piped up again, "Look old thing, I'd like to help. But you've seen the belfry – bats squashed together like sardines! Still, you can squeeze in beside me for a while – till you find something better."

Desmond smiled and thanked his friend.

"By the way," he said. "I'm Desmond."

"Very pleased to meet you, Desmond! My name's Gertie," said Desmond's friend.

So his new friend was female! Desmond blushed. Thank goodness his fur covered him up! They were getting nearer to the town. Desmond could see the headlight beams from cars pulling in and out of the busy petrol station.

"All those people!" said Desmond. "Tell me, Gertie. Something's puzzling me. How come you bats are left alone in peace up there in the belfry?"

"Oh that's easy!" said Gertie, as all the bats settled in the big oak tree in the park on the edge of town. "The vicar likes us! He wouldn't let anyone touch the belfry. Besides – we're an endangered species!"

"Endangered species," echoed Desmond. He'd felt endangered all right when Mrs Best was waving that great sucking beast at him. But that couldn't

be what his bat friend was meaning. Hey! Hadn't
he read something about bats being endangered species in an encyclopaedia when he was a boy in Class
3? He was about to ask Gertie for a few more details,
when something flitted past the end of the branch
where he was hanging. Desmond squinted: tall hat,
long broomstick, cat, cooking pot, big black bag.

"I know who that is!" squeaked Desmond. "And
I bet I know where she's going, too! Goodbye Gertie.
See you later ... I hope. Right now I've got to try
to save that school!"

Without further ado, he flew off into the night,
pinging his way through the darkness, hot on the
broomstick's trail.

9

There was a tinkle of shattering glass.

"She's breaking in!" gasped Desmond in disbelief.

He was hanging inside the cycle shed in the school playground, catching his breath. His wings were aching, for he had chased the witch on the broom-stick right across town and in through the school gates.

"I suppose I'd better go and see what she's up to," he sighed as he slipped from the shadows and flew silently round to the back of the school.

The glass in the little window of the teachers' loo had been smashed and the window-catch had been opened. Desmond glided in and fluttered about over the basin for a moment or two to get his bear-ings. Beyond the open door, to the left, was the main hall and the stairs. On the right the corridor curved away, looking rather spooky by night. Class 3's class-room was round the corner and, for old times' sake, Desmond flapped off towards it.

There was a light on. The witch was rearranging Class 3's desks.

"This is going to suit us very well!" she said to the cat, who sat watching, curled up on Mr Gosling's chair. The broomstick was propped up next to the display board. Desmond noticed the leaflet about Chumley Castle which Mr Gosling had hung there – before the fateful class outing.

Swooping in through the doorway, Desmond hooked himself onto the highest bookshelf on the far side of the room.

"Oh it's you!" said the witch, hardly glancing up from her work. "Changed your mind about coming to live here?"

Without giving Desmond a chance to reply, she began humming as she cleared all the books from the shelves underneath him. She chucked them over her shoulder – Junior Atlases, New Red Maths books, History folders – they all landed in an untidy heap in a corner.

"Mr Gosling will go bananas!" Desmond murmured as the witch blew puffs of dust from her own mouldy books and stood them up on the shelves.

"That's better!" she cackled. "I feel quite settled already. Couldn't be more perfect! It's just what I've been looking for."

Lifting the cat onto her lap, she collapsed happily into Mr Gosling's chair. It swivelled.

"Wheee!" the witch shrieked. "Terrific!"

The cat sprang to safety on Mr Gosling's desk as the witch kicked with her heels, making the chair spin like a top. Desmond remembered Jason doing the very same thing once, when Mr Gosling was out having his coffee break.

"Stop!" squeaked Desmond. "Stop! Listen to me!"

The witch let her feet trail. She glared at Desmond from beneath the brim of her black hat. Gradually the chair stopped spinning.

"Spoilsport!" she said sulkily. "What's the matter now?"

Desmond tried to sound indignant, which is quite difficult when you're squeaking.

"This is a school — not a house!" he said. "It may be empty now, but in the morning there'll be crowds of people. You can't live here!"

"No such thing as can't!" snapped the witch, folding her arms defiantly.

She sounds a bit like a teacher already, thought Desmond.

The witch got up and went to the bookshelf and took down a huge book. "Somewhere in here I've got the perfect spell for making that Enchanted Forest I told you about – fifty metres thick. That'll keep any visitors out! And if anyone did get in, there's always the Hundred Years' Sleep!"

She flicked through the tatty pages.

"Oh dearrr," said the cat wearily. "Dearrr, oh dearrr!" She rubbed her arched back along the edge of the bookcase where Desmond was still hanging. "The trrrouble is she's always losing things. Spells in particularrr! Take the spell that turrrned you into a bat forrr instance. She just happened to come across that one just beforrre you drrropped in. That's why you'rrre a bat and not a frrrog! And I don't suppose she has the foggiest idea how to put it into rrreverrrse! It'll be exactly the same with the Enchanted Forrrest, just you wait and see!"

Desmond, despite his furry coat, felt a chill run right down his spine. A lump in his throat almost stopped him from squeaking.

"What! You mean ... she hasn't got the spell to turn me back into a boy again?"

"Oh she's got it alrrright – sorrrt of," said the cat. "It's just that she will have forrrgotten what page it's on – and what book it's in!"

Meanwhile, the witch had given up looking for the Enchanted Forest spell. Instead she'd spotted the nature table and the tank with the toads. She was dabbling her warty hand amongst the water weeds, making grabs at the terrified beasts.

"See!" she shrieked at Desmond. "I told you this place was just made for me! Everybody knows witches and toads go together."

Desmond felt defeated. As you know, he wasn't much of a hero. He peered sadly and mistily round the class-room thinking of all the members of Class 3 – and of one particular friend. Suddenly he had an idea!

Jason! Of course! Why didn't I think of it before? I'll go and find Jason. He's daring and brave! He'll save the situation! Oh yes! Jason's a real hero!

He squeaked gleefully at the witch, "Just you wait. Jason will soon get the better of you!"

And with that, he flapped out of the class-room, down the shadowy corridor and through the window of the teachers' loo. He flew as hard and as fast as he could, pinging his way between chimney-pots and T.V. aerials, over roof-tops and trees.

Desmond was still reeling from the shock that he might remain a bat for the rest of his life ... but as he flew towards Jason's house he was full of excitement. This is what adventures were all about!

"OK, I may not be a real hero," he said to himself, "but this is my chance to do something brave! I might never get round to doing anything heroic again – but tonight I'm going to save our school!"

Jason's house was Number Five, Sunnybank Drive. Desmond dived down towards it, making for the light that shone from a side window. He knew this was the room that Jason shared with his big brother Terry, and the flickering blue light told him that they were watching T.V.

Desmond took a deep breath. Then, with a mighty squeak, he hurled himself towards the window. The "ping!" shot back, warning him how close he was getting to the glass.

Then, with a slap like a wet wellie, Desmond's right wing flapped against the window pane.

"Jason!" he squeaked. "Jason, it's me! Desmond! This has to be a flying visit! You see – I need your help!"

Terry was just pulling the curtains across the window. He heard – and saw – Desmond, and jumped back, startled.

"Hey, Jason!" Terry called. "There's a bat!"

"No it's not! No it's not!" squeaked Desmond at the top of his voice. "Don't you know me? It's Desmond!"

But Jason couldn't be bothered with bats. The Big Match was about to begin. He dropped a toffee into his mouth and flopped onto the bed.

10

Desmond gave up. He spent the rest of the night hanging from the roof of the shed in Jason's back garden. To begin with, he squinted across the moon-lit grass at the tiny crack in the curtains, where the blue light flickered. He watched until Jason and Terry switched the T.V. off. He guessed the match was over and they were going to bed. It was late. They were tired, unlike Desmond who was still wide awake.

Then a dreadful thought dropped into Desmond's head. Even if he had been able to make Jason see him, he certainly wouldn't have been able to speak to him.

"The fact is I'm a bat instead of a boy!" he told himself. "And a useless bat at that! I know I can talk to a witch – and to a cat – thanks to all that silly magic, but as for making sense to other boys …" Desmond sighed, "I might as well be stuffed, like that bat in Dad's study … wait a minute … the study! Of course!"

An idea flashed like lightning through Desmond's tiny mind – I'll write a note to Jason, explaining everything. It'll be easy, as long as I can get to Dad's word processor!

Desmond hung from the shed, perfecting his plan as best he could. From time to time, he was gripped with fears. What if he couldn't get inside his house?

What if he couldn't get the word processor going? And worse ... what if Jason decided he liked the idea of their school being lost for a hundred years? Desmond shivered and told himself firmly that heroes didn't worry about such things. A pink glow began spreading over the sky. The new day was beginning. Taking a deep breath, Desmond launched himself from the shed and made a bee-line, or rather a bat-line, straight back to his old home.

Once there, he did a quick circuit to see if any windows were open and noticed that the one into the study was most certainly closed. There was a peaceful hush about the place. Everybody was sleeping. Well, nearly everybody, for Desmond had spotted that the kitchen door was open. Celine was sitting at the kitchen table eating toast, while Sam played with the remains of last night's supper in the cat's bowl. Good old Sam! He always woke up early!

Suddenly Celine sprang to her feet and with an "Oo la la!" grabbed Sam, who was stuffing handfuls of cold lasagne into his mouth. At the same time, Desmond seized his chance. While Sam was yelling, he skimmed noiselessly overhead, through the kitchen, into the hall and up two flights of stairs.

For once, luck was with him. The door to the study was open and Desmond flew straight over to the desk.

"Find a pencil! There must be a pencil somewhere!" he muttered. The idea was to use the pencil

to flick the "on" switch on the word processor –
and then to fly carefully at the keys.

Desmond scanned the room short-sightedly.
Below him were all the cases crammed full of insects.
He used to think they looked revolting but now,
as he caught sight of all those fluffy moths and
crunchy beetles, he could feel his mouth watering.
They all looked rather delicious! Then he noticed
he was flying over the case where the stuffed bat
hung from its stick. And his eyes chanced upon the
label on the case:

"GREATER HORSESHOE BAT – ENDANGERED SPECIES"

"There it is again," squeaked Desmond. "Must
try and find out what it means."

"Eeek! Eeek!" someone cried down below him.

Desmond squinted and recognized Sam. He was pointing to the ceiling. He grinned and flapped his arms and pointed again. I wonder, thought Desmond, does he recognize me?

From the lampshade in the middle of the ceiling, Desmond hung and watched while Sam began constructing a sort of ladder. First he put a footstool onto a chair. Next he dragged two big books from a shelf and, staggering back, piled them on top of the stool. Then he began to climb.

"Oh heck!" panicked Desmond. "He's trying to get to me!"

Almost immediately, Sam's "ladder" began to wobble. He was only half way up when, with an

almighty CLATTER the whole lot went crashing to the floor. Sam sat screaming in the middle – not hurt, but angry. But as the door to the study was flung open and Celine rushed in, Sam stopped yelling and started squealing and pointing to the ceiling.

"What ees eet, cheri? What 'ave you been trying to reach?" said Celine. She followed Sam's finger and looked up. Then she screamed: "Une chauve-souris! une chauve-souris!" (which actually means a bald mouse and is – for some reason – the French for a bat.)

Within seconds, doors were opening and voices were calling, "What is it?" "What's happened?" "Where are you Celine?"

Desmond saw his dad fumbling with his glasses. His mum had her hair-rollers in. His big brother came out of the bathroom wrapped in a towel and scowling.

But it was his big sister who called, "Hey everyone! Desmond's missing!"

When the whole family, including Sam and Celine, crowded into his old bedroom to look, Desmond made his escape. He flew out through the bathroom window (which his brother had opened to get rid of the steam) and off between the houses towards the trees.

Trembling all over, Desmond huddled himself tightly and hung from one of the highest branches of the conker tree at the end of the street. What about the word processor? What about the note?

"Failed again!" said Desmond unhappily, "What a hero!" and a tear rolled down his furry cheek.

He must have been hanging there, half-dozing, half-moping, for ages, when a voice spoke to him from between the leaves.

"Is that you, Desmond?" it asked. "I've been looking for you everywhere! It's me – Gertie. And I've brought some friends – Pip and Squeak!"

Desmond peered at the bats hanging from the next branch.

"Gertie?" he said. "What are you doing here?"

"Well, you know what you were telling us about your problems at the castle? And about the witch's rather drastic, not to mention impractical, plan to live in the school?" squeaked Desmond's friend.

Desmond nodded his furry head.

"So, guess what? We've had a wonderful idea! Come closer and I'll whisper it in your ear."

A few minutes later, Desmond and Gertie and Pip and Squeak were flying into the dazzling morning sunlight. They flew without a sound over the churning rush-hour traffic on the road below. If anyone looked up and saw them, they mistook them for birds.

"Not much further!" puffed Desmond. "Just another two streets. The first thing you'll see is the playground and the big iron gates . . . HEY!"

Desmond stopped suddenly, as if he'd slammed on his brakes.

"It's too late!" he cried. "It's happened! That's my old school down there – but there's a huge forest right round it!"

11

"Oh heck!" said Desmond. "She's done it! She must have found the spell! I just hope that forest started to grow before Mr Gosling rang the morning bell and not after ... or else everyone will be trapped!"

The four bats circled the school. The red rooftops were just peeping out from among the trees. The rest was lost in the deepest, darkest part of the Enchanted Forest.

"Whatever can we do?" Desmond squeaked. There were a lot of other people wondering the very same thing. A crowd had gathered outside the

forest. Three police cars, their doors open, were parked by the edge of the trees. The policemen were clustered together, muttering and scratching their heads. Someone had called the fire brigade. The largest wagon had its ladder extended and five firemen with axes were hacking at the trees from above and below.

"It's no good, Joe!" one of them called. "It's hopeless! Whenever we get a hole made, it grows over again!"

Desmond noticed a few shreds of clothing tangled among the thorns and briars. A few brave passers-by had obviously had a go at cutting a way through. They didn't stand a chance though. There was nothing anyone could do.

Overhead a helicopter flew round and round, buzzing like a puzzled dragonfly. There was nowhere for it to land – the school playground had disappeared under a blanket of thick greenery.

Then Desmond had an idea.

"Come on!" he called. "Follow me!"

With all the excitement, no one noticed four bats flying over the forest, then diving low somewhere round the back of the school. Desmond led his friends in and out of the branches, close over the cycle shed and through the open window of the teachers' loo.

It was eerily silent inside, and gloomy too. The sun hardly broke through the trees. Thickly-leaved branches pressed against the window panes.

"This way!" said Desmond, flying as fast as he could round the corner to Class 3. Reaching the class-room door, the things that he saw with his short-sighted eyes made him gasp with horror.

The desks were all occupied. Every member of Class 3 was in his or her place – some sitting, some standing, some half-way in between. Every face had a peaceful, smiling expression. And everyone was perfectly still, like little statues, fast asleep!

Jason was there, of course. His arm was raised, ruler at the ready. Desmond guessed he was frozen in the middle of flicking paper pellets at Mr Gosling's back.

Mr Gosling! Desmond gasped again. He had never seen his teacher looking quite like this. He was standing at the front of the class-room, his hand poised, ready to write something on the board.

Desmond could imagine him saying, "All right! All right! Settle down Class 3!"

But Mr Gosling was in such a deep sleep, that as Desmond flew round and round his bald head, all he could hear was the gentle rise and fall of his teacher's snoring.

Of course, the witch and the cat were there enjoying a late breakfast. They were using Mr Gosling's desk as their table.

"Where've you been then?" the witch asked Desmond, wiping her hands on her dress. "There's not much breakfast left. But I've noticed a few spiders in the corners round here, and a few dried-up specimens, locusts and the like, over there."

She nodded towards the nature table. Desmond had a feeling that the toads were missing. He had an idea too that the witch's breakfast was a messy brownish-green!

"Poor things!" he murmured as he and his three friends flew over to the bookshelves.

Hanging there, Desmond took a deep breath and said to the witch, "OK, we've had enough of this. And when everyone gets through that forest you're going to be in a lot of trouble! Kidnapping they call it. Or in this case classnapping. And the teacher too! Oh I wouldn't be in your shoes for anything!"

But the witch simply cackled, 'Ha! Who cares! Anyway, bats don't wear shoes! And I can't see this lot doing much to shift me, can you? As for the rest of them – they can't catch me! They'll never cut through that forest, not in a hundred years!"

Then Gertie nudged Desmond, and whispered, "Go on. Tell her about the plan! You remember! Endangered Species!"

Desmond nodded. The witch had begun to empty the black cooking pot into the sink. There was a dreadful pong – right next to Mr Gosling. But he didn't seem at all bothered.

"Listen!" said Desmond. "I thought you liked

peace and quiet?"

"I do!" snapped the witch. She grinned at Mr Gosling and Class 3, "they're not very noisy now, are they?"

"Maybe not," agreed Desmond, "but out there they've got the police and the fire brigade. Next it'll be the army! And even if they can't get in, just think of all the tourists who'll want to come and see! A hundred years or not – they'll never leave you in peace!"

The witch did appear to be thinking about this as she piled up the dirty dishes, so Desmond went on, "And did you know that bats are an endangered species?"

"What's that got to do with it?" scowled the witch.

"Come with me!" said Desmond, "and you'll soon see!"

He flew out of the class-room and along the corridor to the school library.

The witch hurried after him, shrieking, "If this is a trick, you'll be endangered all right!"

All the same she followed Desmond and Gertie and Pip and Squeak into the library. Desmond flew up and down the rows of books, squinting hard. He was looking for the section marked "NATURE".

"Here!" he squeaked suddenly. "Take a look at this!"

With one wing, he flapped frantically at a big thick encyclopaedia. It was the one he'd copied all the bits out of for his project on "Creatures of the Night".

The witch eyed him suspiciously as she heaved it from the shelf. She opened it on a table and began turning the pages slowly.

"Find the bit about conservation," said Desmond, fluttering anxiously. "There – 'Species in Danger'. Now, go on, read!"

12

"**T**his is all very well," sighed the witch. "Bats may be special creatures. And their homes may be protected. But is one bat enough?" She glared at Desmond. "Because that's all I've got – and it's a pretty useless bat at that!"

Desmond sniffed, ignoring the insult. He waved a wing towards his three friends who were hanging from the big library lampshade.

"We've got a plan," he explained. "These bats live in the church belfry – all squeezed in together with lots more like them. There's a real overcrowding problem! At least thirty, maybe fifty, might be

persuaded to move in with you ... if you promise to be nice."

"Persuaded?!" the witch began to splutter. "Nice?"

But Desmond cut in with: "Not here though. Somewhere much better! I mean, let's be honest. You're not really going to be happy here are you? It's not grotty enough, is it? Or creepy? So why not move back to the castle, and take lots of bats back with you?"

It took a moment or so for the idea to sink in. Then the witch shrieked, "Brilliant! It's brilliant! It'll fix that Mrs Best and her committee! If my room in the castle is stuffed full of bats, there's nothing anyone can do! They'll have to leave us in peace!"

She grinned at Desmond.

"Endangered species eh? Perhaps you're not such a useless little beast after all!"

She did a dance three times round the library table and, still cackling, skipped back down the corridor to Class 3's class-room.

"Get packing!" she yelled at the cat as she flung their belongings – cooking pot, cooking stove, books – into the black bag. "Nasty modern building! Never liked it anyway." She glanced at the sleeping Mr Gosling. "What sort of a creature would want to spend his time in here every day!"

The cat sprang up onto Mr Gosling's shoulder to take a closer look.

"Verrry strrrange! Verrry strrrange!" she purred.

Mr Gosling didn't bat an eyelid as the cat's tail slid across his face. Surely the witch wasn't going to leave him like that, was she?

"Hey! Before you leave," squeaked Desmond, "what about the forest? And all this lot?"

"Oh yes," said the witch, "I almost forgot."

She rummaged about in her bag while the cat looked knowingly at Desmond.

"Now then," muttered the witch. "Which book was it ... ?"

"I told you so." said the cat smugly. "Perrrfectly drrreadful memorrry!"

Suddenly the witch fastened her bag – with the books inside.

"Can't be bothered!" she declared. "I'll try again another time!"

Another time? Desmond wondered. What does she mean. Next day? Next week?? Next century???

With a grin and a wave, the witch hopped onto the broomstick and glided out of the class-room. She zoomed down the corridor. Gertie, Pip and Squeak flew after her. But at the doorway to the teachers' loo she turned and called to Desmond, who had not followed his friends.

"What about you then? Coming?"

Desmond shook his little furry head.

"I think I'll stay here with my old friends," he squeaked. "Thanks all the same."

The witch shrugged. "Suit yourself!" she replied. And then to Gertie, Pip and Squeak who were flapping next to the broomstick she said: "Come on you lot. We'll call in at the belfry and collect some more recruits!"

So Desmond settled himself, hanging from the window-frame next to his old desk. As the silent minutes ticked by, he couldn't help thinking that, apart from the things that had happened to him, this could have been any old morning. Here was Class 3 happily snoozing, as usual. It just needed Mr Gosling to be droning on about something ...

Suddenly there was a BANG! and a FLASH! and sunlight came flooding back into the class-room as the forest shrank to nothing! Desmond landed in his desk.

Someone was calling him: "Desmond! Desmond? Are you day-dreaming again?"

Mr Gosling cuffed him on the ear. Desmond lifted his hand. No wings! No fur!

"What?... Eh?... Sorry sir?" he said. Of course! The witch had found the spell and turned him back into a boy again!

"Where's your absence note then?" said Mr Gosling.

Desmond sat back and fiddled with his glasses.

"Hey!" Jason said. "Ask Desmond if he knows what happened to those toads, sir. He sits next to their tank, perhaps he's had them for a snack!"

Class 3 giggled, but Desmond wasn't listening. Out of the corner of his eye he noticed the History folders, the New Red Maths books and the Junior Atlases in an untidy pile beside the bookshelf.

"Should I tell them?" he wondered, "about Bat Boy? And the cat? And the witch?... No point really, they'd never believe it!"

So Desmond sighed and shrugged.

"Well, Desmond?" said Mr Gosling. "What have you been up to?"

"Me sir?" said Desmond. "Oh ... nothing much."